MW01047085

Buddy the Blue Corgi

Good Things Take Time

Written by Suzanna Lynn

Illustrated by Suzanna Smith

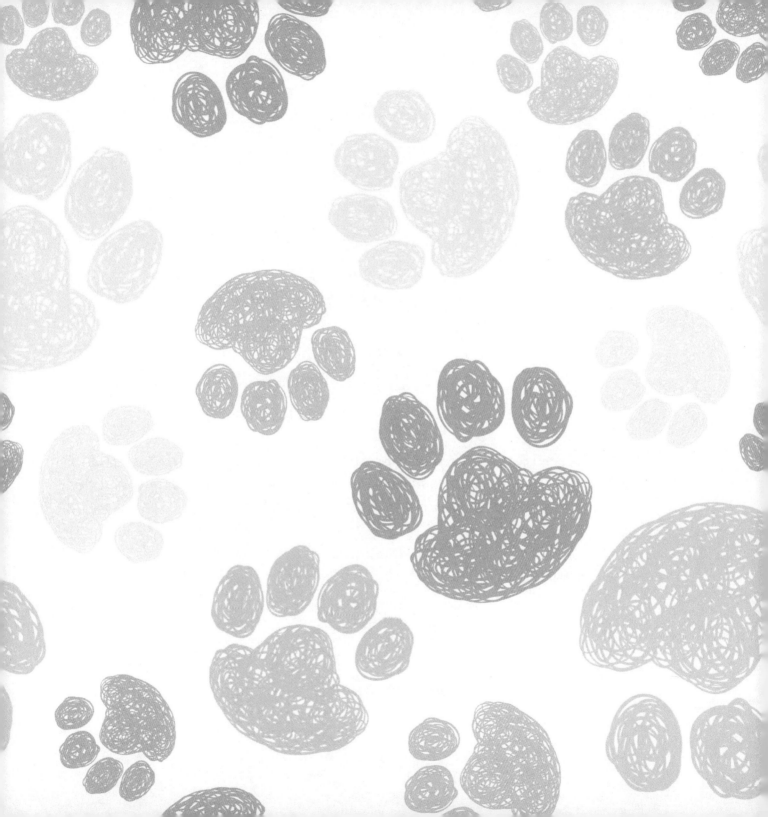

Buddy the Blue Corgi – Good Things Take Time

All rights reserved. Any unauthorized reprint or use of this material is strictly prohibited. No part of this book may be reproduced or transmitted in any form without express written permission from the author except for the use of brief quotations in a book review.

Copyright © 2020 by Suzanna Lynn. All rights reserved.
Published by Lil Pumpkins Publishing, PO Box 755, Seymour, MO 65746.

Edited by Hollie the Editor
Illustration and design by Suzanna Smith

ISBN - 978-1-956079-05-0

<u>*Dedication:*</u>

To Mima Ted, for always believing in me,
even when I didn't believe in myself.

My name's Buddy the Blue Corgi. These are my brothers, Donut and Salem.

What's that? We don't look alike? Well, that's because we're all adopted. I remember when I was waiting to be adopted. I thought the day would never come.

I was born on a farm in Kansas. I was one of five puppies, and our mother, Maddie, loved us very much.

As we grew, my brothers and sisters and I would spend our days playing around the farm. We loved chasing the ducks and napping in the haystacks.

One day while playing, we noticed some strangers looking at us. They were talking to the farmer.

"Who are those people?" I asked Momma.
"Why do they keep looking at us?"

Momma gave a sad smile. "My sweet boy,
it will be time for you to be adopted soon."

"Adopted?" my sister Winnie asked. "What is adopted?"

"Adopted means that someday one of those people may take you home with them," Momma explained. "They will be your new family."

At first, we were very scared of the idea. None of us wanted to leave the farm. But when Momma explained that we would get a new family and have new adventures, I began to get excited.

Each day new people would come to look at us. Some were older with white fur on top of their heads. Others were families that had little kids to play with.

Then one day, a little boy came and took my sister Millie home with him.

We were all very sad to see her go.

"Don't be sad, my little ones," Momma said. "Millie has gone to her forever home! That little boy will care for her, play with her, and they will be best friends forever."

I liked the idea of a forever home. So, each day I sat patiently, waiting for my family to arrive.

The next day, a man and woman came. I was sure it would be my day. I wagged my tail and yipped and yapped to show them just how fun I would be.

"What about that one?" asked the man, pointing to me.

"The blue one with the tail?" asked the woman. "No, I want my puppy to look like the other tan ones."

I was sad. I knew I was different, but Momma taught me that God made me different, and that I'm special. So, I kept waiting. I was sure I would find my forever family soon.

But each family that came ended up picking one of the other puppies.

Soon, it was just me and Momma left.

That night, I curled up next to Momma. "Why doesn't anybody want to adopt me?"

"It's just not your time," explained Momma. "Don't you worry. The right family will find you and love you."

It had been several days since my brothers and sisters had been adopted, and I had started to lose hope. It wasn't nearly as fun to chase the ducks by myself.

Then, one day, a man and woman showed up. The woman ran straight for me and scooped me up.

"Oh, honey, he's perfect!" she cried to the man. "And he's the most beautiful blue color I've ever seen!" She held me close as I licked her chin.

The man scratched my head. "Yes, he's perfect!"

After I said goodbye to Momma and the farmer, the couple took me with them on a long car ride. I heard them talking, and they had driven three hours and into another state just to pick me. I was that special to them.

When we arrived at the house, there was a bed, a bowl of food, lots of toys, and three little kids waiting for me! The kids petted and kissed me, so I kissed them back.

I got to meet my new big brothers,
Donut and Salem too!

I had a whole family to love and be loved by.

You see, I was so worried that I wouldn't find a home, when really my family just hadn't arrived yet.

Do you get frustrated waiting? Do you feel like things just aren't happening fast enough?

Let's see what the Bible says about it.

"For I know the plans I have for you," declares the Lord, "plans to prosper you and not to harm you, plans to give you hope and a future." —Jeremiah 29:11

So, you see, sometimes waiting can be hard, and even make you sad, but if you're patient and trust in God, it will turn out wonderful.

Did you enjoy this book?

If so, be sure to go leave an honest review on Amazon to let the author know!

Buddy at 8 weeks old   Buddy's PAW-tograph!   Buddy at 10 years old

Buddy the Blue Corgi lives in the deep rolling hills of southwest Missouri with his mommy, Author Suzanna Lynn.

One day while watching her children play outside with Buddy, Suzanna thought about how many lessons Buddy had learned in his life—from feeling different to learning to get along with new friends. She realized these were trials kids, including her own, go through every day.

After much prayer and planning, she began writing the Buddy the Blue Corgi stories. These stories are designed to help children understand and work through everyday problems.

Made in the USA
Middletown, DE
30 October 2024

63568629R00027